Tucker Finds His Forever Home

Written by
Beth Cherryholmes Miller, founder of Wagtown,
a nonprofit organization that helps communities
become more dog friendly.

Watercolor Artwork by
Erica Schindler

ISBN: 978-1-09834-788-8

Dear dog lover,

Thank you! With the purchase of each book, you support Wagtown's charitable work to help create dog-friendly communities. I wrote this book to help children better understand dogs and to inspire them to be a champion for animals. 100% of the proceeds from "Tucker Finds His Forever Home" go to programs and projects that create a better world for dogs.

Wagtown is a nonprofit that works with communities across the United States that want to be more dog friendly. We provide the expertise that is the bridge between "we want to be dog friendly" and "we are dog friendly." Wagtown's vision is to create communities where you can enjoy authentic and responsible dog friendliness.

The impact of dog friendliness is astonishing. Communities that welcome dogs are more committed to animal welfare, more responsible with their dogs, safer, healthier, more welcoming with places for dogs, and more economically vibrant. These outcomes create benefits for the entire community.

To achieve our mission, we help leaders and grassroots organizations pursue dog friendliness with a variety of programs and projects. Your involvement is crucial, so thank you again for your purchase. The evolution toward more dog-friendly communities begins with each of us. We can make a difference. Dogs make the world a better place. Now it's time to make the world a better place for dogs.

To follow our journey and see how you can get involved in making your community more dog friendly, visit www.wagtown.org.

Keep wagging,

Beth Miller, Founder of Wagtown

Dedicated to all those
who make the wag happen.

Under a tree in a very big park lies a sleeping puppy who is just waking up. Tucker sniffs the air and opens one eye. *Where am I? Where is Henry?* thinks the puppy. *What am I doing here??!* Then the puppy remembers. Henry took him for a car ride to the park. Tucker thought they were going to play. But instead, Henry started crying and left Tucker all alone, tied to a tree with a strong rope. "Goodbye, Tucker," Henry said, crying, as he walked away.

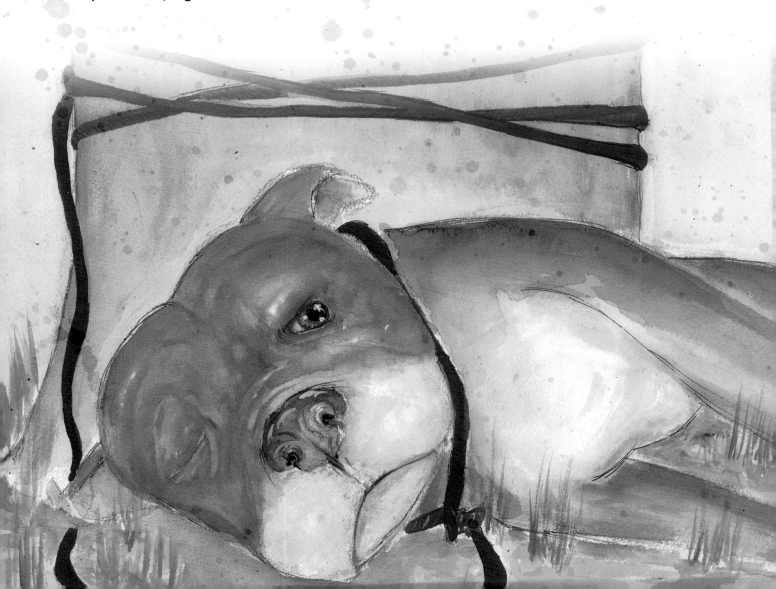

Tucker jumps up and tries to run. He forgot he is tied to a tree. The rope stops Tucker, and he tumbles to the ground. He starts barking and lunging, desperate to get away. Then Tucker begins to howl. Aaaaarrrrrroooooo! Aaaaaarrrrrrrrroooooooooohhhhhhh!

What is wrong with me? wonders
Tucker. *Why is everyone afraid of me?*
Tucker feels sad and alone. He's tired.
He's thirsty. And he's hungry. But he's
tied to a tree and can't get away.

It's getting dark, and the night air is chilly. Tucker is cold and wants to find a warm place to take a nap, but the rope is tight around his neck. Then Tucker has an idea... he starts chewing and chewing and chewing. Finally, the rope is broken, and Tucker is free!

Cold and exhausted, Tucker finds an empty box in an alley where he falls asleep. He dreams of his soft, fluffy bed. He dreams of Henry. And he dreams of his old home.

The next morning, Tucker awakens to a man in a uniform with a soft voice. "Hey little guy," the man says, "I'm taking you to the shelter where you'll get water, treats and a nice, fluffy bed." Tucker is so happy! Finally, he will find his forever home. Or will he? He overhears the man in the uniform say Tucker might not be adoptable because of the way he looks. *No one wants me*, Tucker thinks.

Tucker's first day at the shelter is full of new things. A new cage with a fluffy bed! His own water bowl! Chow two times a day! A new stuffed monkey toy! And even a bath! Tucker is feeling hopeful. He believes he will be adopted.

Tucker has a plan. He will be the best-behaved dog in the shelter. Every time he sees someone coming down his aisle, he sits up straight in his cage. He wags his tail. He smiles as big as he can. But no one stops at his cage. They walk right by him. Some say, "We don't want a pit mix. They are mean dogs."

Several weeks pass and Tucker's happiness is fading. Many of the dogs around Tucker have been adopted. Rocky, a big black lab, went to his forever home with a fireman. Holly, a sassy little terrier mix with a big puff of hair on her head, went home with a little old lady. Even Boone, an old hound dog with a deep howl, left with a family that lives on a farm. Sad and caged, even Tucker's favorite toy, his stuffed monkey, can't cheer him up.

One day Tucker is curled up in the corner of his cage. He is watching Popcorn, the curly brown poodle, being led away from her cage. Another dog gets a forever home, thinks Tucker. Little tears trickle down Tucker's nose. He buries his head in his fluffy bed.

Suddenly, Tucker looks up and sees a nice woman standing at his cage. This must be a dream, Tucker thinks. No one has ever stopped at my cage. The woman, whose name is Lyla, smiles at Tucker and touches his nose. Tucker smiles back and wags his tail.

Lyla takes Tucker outside to the fenced play area. She walks Tucker around the yard. She throws a ball and Tucker catches it. She calls Tucker and he runs to her. Tucker and Lyla are so happy together.

Tucker is finally being adopted! Lyla tells Tucker that she is taking him on a very long car ride. They are going to a place where dogs are not judged by the way they look or by what people say about them. Lyla says "This will be a place that you will love, Tucker! There are lots of dogs that live here."

Tucker is excited to see this new kind of town. Lyla called it a "Wagtown Community," where dog owners are responsible and dogs are treated like a part of the family. Tucker peeks over the front seat and sees a big sign that reads "Welcome to a dog-friendly community where all breeds are welcome."

Finally, Tucker is "home." He sees a big welcome sign on the front door of the townhouse. He sees a big bone with a red ribbon tied around it. He sees a nice, green shady spot in the yard with a tree. For a moment, Tucker wonders if he will be tied to that tree and left alone. Soon, though, Tucker puts that thought to rest. He will no longer spend his days tied to a tree!

This makes Tucker feel so wonderful. Tucker sees all kinds of dogs at his new home. He sees big dogs and small dogs. Dogs with pointed ears and dogs with floppy ears. Dogs with bows on their heads and dogs with bandannas. Service dogs and watch dogs. But they all have something in common: they all have collars and tags, they all have their shots, and they know how to sit, make new friends, shake hands, and roll over. Tucker wants to be like these dogs. He wants to learn how to do these tricks.

Lyla takes Tucker to a training class. He learns new tricks and gets praise and treats.

Tucker sees dogs on and off leashes. He
sees a man picking up poop. He sees dogs
greeting each other as their owners take
them for a walk. Everyone is happy –
especially the dogs.

And then Tucker sees another dog who looks just like him. *Another dog like me,*
Tucker thinks. Tucker sees the dog being petted and loved by his owner. He gazes up
at Lyla and she says "You're safe here, Tucker. We accept you just the way you are. I
think you are perfect!" He realizes that maybe he isn't a worthless dog after all.

Lessons from "Tucker Finds His Forever Home"

We shouldn't judge anyone by the way they look or
because of what people say about them.

Being different is okay.

We should accept and respect individuals
for who they are.

It didn't matter what Tucker looks like, he deserves
to be loved and cared for.

In the end, Tucker found out that being himself
was good enough.

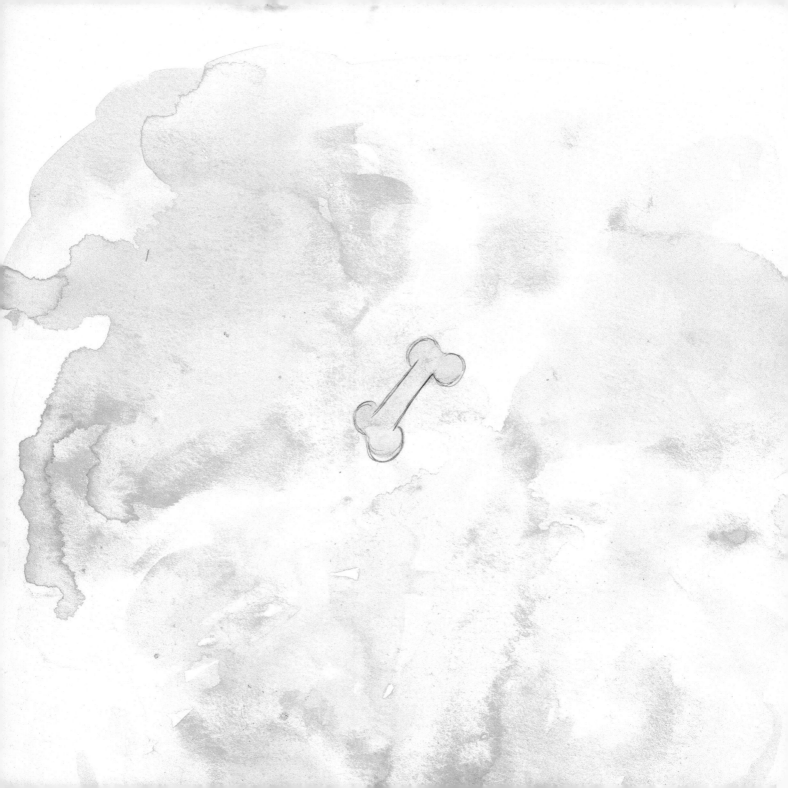